About the Authors

My name is Claudia and I am a Nurse Practitioner by profession. I have two daughters who are now quite grown. Before I became a nurse, I worked as a nanny, I later became a substitute teacher and volunteered to teach children of all ages. Now as a Nurse Practitioner I continue to work with children as well as their families.

Lumpy Socks

To Shayla, Rowan,
May you grow up and change
your world..

Claudia Martial

Lumpy Socks

Olympia Publishers
London

www.olympiapublishers.com

OLYMPIA PAPERBACK EDITION

A CIP catalogue record for this title is
available from the British Library.

ISBN: 978-1-78830-500-6

This story is purely fiction and the names used does not represent or belong to
anyone or person.

First Published in 2020

Olympia Publishers
Tallis House
2 Tallis Street
London
EC4Y 0AB
Printed in Great Britain

Dedication

To every child, may their smile and laughter continue to inspire us.

Acknowledgements

All my children

Gabby was four years old and she had big brown eyes and curly black hair.

It was the end of spring and Gabby was getting
ready to go out to play.
"I HATE LUMPY SOCKS!" she shouted.

"I have never heard of such a thing," said Mom.
She turned the socks over.
"I don't see any Lumps."

"Maybe they fell out and rolled under the bed," said Gabby.

But when she looked, she did not find any lumps.

Mom put her arms around Gabby and said softly,
"We wear socks to keep our feet warm."
"But they don't feel good if they're lumpy!"
said Gabby.

"In the fall when you played with the leaves and went trick or treating, you wore your pumpkin socks," said Mom. "Were there any lumps in those socks?"

"No!" said Gabby with a giggle.
"I like my Halloween socks."

"In the winter when it snowed you wore thick woolly socks," said Mom.
"Were there any lumps in those socks?"

"No!" said Gabby. "And I love my woolly socks because they keep me warm when I'm making a snowman."

"In the spring you wore your pink and yellow socks," continued Mom. "Were there lumps in those socks?"

Gabby smiled.
"No. Pink socks make me feel so pretty."

"Soon it will be summer, it will be warm, and you will be able to wear your sandals," said Mom with a smile.

"And no socks!" said Gabby,
jumping up and down.

Gabby liked summer best of all because she could wear her sandals. She could splash around in puddles and could see her toes wiggle.

"But when will it be summer?" Gabby whined. "It feels like it will never come."

Mom opened the door. The sun was bright, and it felt very warm. "Guess what," said Mom. "It's the first day of summer! You can wear your sandals today!"

Gabby cheered, slipped on her sandals and skipped outside. She was very happy.

Because it was summer.

9 781788 305006